MW00940492

Nicewood
Imagined

"Minds unfunkable... forever never end."

Dave and John

Copyright © 2002 by Brian Schoenholtz,
Gainesville, Florida 32653

Cora, Mace

The Land of Dawny Dusk: Pirate

www.macecora.com

nicewoodimagined@yahoo.com

Nicewood Imagined

ISBN: 0-9720334-2-4
Printed in Hong Kong
10 9 8 7 6 5 4 3 2 1

"Welcome once more to an astonishing tale,
I was hoping the others would not ignorantly fail,
and I'm pleased that they didn't, or I'd be all done,
spitting stories at children who just love it a ton.
And what do ya know, but again you're in luck,
for Brayton dripped paint so one more
story I'll pluck,
from this Dawny Dusk land so tremen-
dously grand,
where the Northern West sun is liable to tan.
So keep your eyes shaded as we hunt
over dunes,
through turquoise-cream waters for scav-
enging loons.
"But wait, what's that smell?" quipped a Bentleyville crow.
"But wait to yourself because I betcha I know,
just follow this story over trade windy blows,
and unbolt your nose to where the scent goes,
for there's a barbeque that's roasting on fairy-tale flames,
where a Loodoodle sizzles fish amidst green Googin games.
So are you all ready? Are you ready to go?
Just let me ready myself. Now…ready…set…go!"
A sensuous aroma drifted thick through the sky,
as Tuffo diced mushrooms that had overnight dried,
which nimbly he flicked on some rainbow meat fish,
like the windsurfing stik who had taught him the dish.
and though he did cook with one absent, patched eye,
three Hali-butts were sandwiched between tart, marble rye.
One for a surfer, a creature named Tarry,
who could carve mammoth waves without thinking it scary,

2

and a drop of blazed pepper sat soaked on his bread,
'cause he liked how the spices spin-spun in his head.
Two was for Waxel, by the first name of Moon,
who grew up secluded in the town of Dhahroon,
where kite-boarding was in, of which he was the man,
the number one rider in Dawny Dusk's desert land.
And his sandwich was drenched in poppyseed mustard,
with a spoonful of mango, and some curdling custard,
for Moon liked the taste that made others gag,
but most thought he ate it just for reason to brag.
Three was for Tuffo, who had cooked these fine treats,
while Tarry and Waxel had charged this Sea's outer reef,
and he half-sliced the sandwiches in order to eat,
while punting aside Googins who begged at his feet.
"But Tuffo, please Tuffo, we fancy some scraps,
for we just got released from our seashell jail traps,
and the thought of some Hali on sweet-smelling bread,
has made us all silly since the scent hit our heads!"
"But can you behave?" Tuffo chimed back,
"Would you be silent if I cut you some slack?"
"Yes, of course we'll be good, we most certainly pledge,
we'll take our small scraps and lounge on that ledge,
and mind our own business while you and your pals feast,
on those sandwiches prepared with blue raspberry yeast."
Quite patiently they watched, with drool dripping from lips,
as Tuffo dropped a few morsels like dollar bill tips,
but scramble they did as they fought for the meat,
while not being silent as they'd promised to be.
So Tuffo grabbed up a shell from the baking, white beach,
and blew through its spout for a lesson he'd teach,

to the unruly Googins who gazed up in shock,
as the spell that he cast gathered them back to their block.
"I hope you're all full because I've sentenced you now,
to four days in the shell with not a dry towel."
"Aiiee! Aiiee!" they so hysterically screamed,
while making more promises about how good they would be,
but the walls of the shell were like banana milk oil,
so down they did slip, as their freedom did spoil,
and along the whole way they cursed the prince fish,
that had taught this "jail" spell to any creature that wished.
Well about that same time Tarry and Moon had arrived,
and collapsed where their lunch sat, which they hungrily eyed.
"Welcome my friends, how were your rides?"
Did you shred aqua tubes or do backdoor slides?"
asked Tuffo to the pair as they
shook out their hair,
while gulping down juice
squeezed straight from a pear.
"Dang heck my good pal, you
missed a good time,
we charged ten foot waves and
surfed foamy lime,
but thanks for this meal you so
eagerly made,

for tomorrow it's your turn like our turn surfing today."
And before they could laugh three sandwiches were done,
and the effects of the Hali had just then begun,
while rainbow-dyed juices seeped over the ground,
under yellow-fluffed clouds that now crowded around.
Then down drooped their eyelids over colors that swirled,

as the barbeque campsite now dizzily twirled,
and pass out three did as they bounced to the ground,
only to wake up in a new scene around.
No longer did they sleep on a pasty, shelled shore,
but on a pile of rocks, which they soon did explore,
and carved in the stones were three words flawlessly spelled,
the brand of that place, "Makena Wish Well."
And at the tip of the top they peeked over the edge,
upon some misty, pink water beneath a cliff-hanging ledge,
and Moon swiped an acorn, which he lightly flicked down,
into the rippling well where it noiselessly drowned,
and it wasn't a moment before out popped a whale,
with black on his back and a purple-finned tale.
"Jolly crud did you wish that my brilliant, young friend?"
asked Tarry from a rock where his body did bend.
"Why yes, that I did, my wonderful bud…
now let us go join him and play in the mud!"
So off came their clothes and in pounced the three,
as they dove with the whale in Makena Wish Sea,
amid twinkling bubbles and puffer-faced fish,
and an egotistical seahorse who blew them a kiss.
One by next one, they held out their breath,
until a contest it became to see who was best.
But after a bit their lungs begged for more air,
so they took a short breather in an oxygen lair.
And then up they did swim like a green dolphin gang,
through the warm-blooded water, past a starfish who sang,
but when they emerged, their surroundings had swayed,
into a picturesque cave where a harp stringer played.
"Mellow Mood" was the tune that the creature ripped out,

5

so they all took a seat and the strings they did count.
One hundred there were, all flickering in gold,
upon which were plucked by the fingers quite old,
of a skinny, bald chap with a beard that did drag,
all grayed at the end, on a face that did sag.
"Hello my young friends, how was your trip?"
he said to the kids through crackling lips.
"Looppie Lip Lip Hooray, is all we can say,
you're a brilliant musician and it's an astonishing day!"
And they looked at the harpist in a trance-dizzy daze,
while their five dazzled eyes became peacefully dazed,
and he passed out cigars of a Cuban made type,
which he lit with a spell while he roasted his pipe.
The cool afternoon was spent rhyming off tales,
like the sort that Mace tells but with slow-crawling snails,
until their chestnut-thick smoke had blurred up the place,
which had attracted a pirate with a weasel white face.
"Hey, you jazzed fools, you're spoiling my plans,
for I'm searching for treasure in this Dawny Dusk land,
and the smoke from your cigars and twisted, long pipe,
has clouded my vision for it's just not my type,
so extinguish those cherries and step to the side,
or join my parade to find this fortune that hides."
"Well Mister Harpist I guess that's our cue,
for we like telling stories but we like treasure too,
we had such a grand time, and we hope you don't stop,
stringing cheese music for it's much better than Pop!"
Well then they shook hands with their talented friend,
and followed the white weasel around the next bend,
into a flowering garden with quarry stone rocks,

where the weasel-like pirate gave them Vaseline-like socks.
"Here…these will help…in your search of this place,
to glide across grass with a skunk style taste,
so stretch out your toes as you bring up the flank,
and don't fall on your face, or you'll walk candy cane plank!"
But a pin dropped in silence as his
voice echoed out,
for everyone had gone quiet at
the sound of his spout,
you see, one must first learn that
Loodoodles are prideful,
so barking out orders proves only to be spiteful.
And Tuffo with one eye was the first to respond,
as they stood by a melon patch near a crystal green pond.
"Well what are we looking for, you dastardly fiend?
You say we're looking for treasure but what do you mean?"
"Ok…I am sorry," he replied with a frown,
"we're looking for a map in this flower-dripped town,
and on it there'll be an "x"-marking spot,
that shows us the site of our treasure chest plot."
So split up they did into the garden of lush,
through tomato patch rows and soils of mush.
And it wasn't too long before Moon found a clue,
an orange-dripped map stained with purple fruit juice,
which led them to search the blackberry thicket,
after stopping for water at a streaming well spicket.
But after being pricked like twenty-five times,
Tarry confronted the pirate with this questioning rhyme.
"Hey weasel, do you even have the proper credentials,
to be searching for treasure so top confidential?"

"Well that's a good question so let me explain,
for you're covered in thorns which are causing you pain.
I was informed of this wealth by a pink-bellied monkey,
who had been drunk on some nectar, like a honeycomb junkie,
so he spilled his whole guts to me that full moony night,
which included directions to this exact garden sight."
And the pirate then pointed with a long finger down,
to a crayon drawn path, which started in brown,
and all of them followed it through a quarter cent toll,
which placed them in front of a dignified troll,
who stood by an orange-colored, vine-covered wall,
by a stony arched doorway with a rainbow wide hall.
"Well howdy ya' all, I see you finally arrived,
what took you so long, was it that fluttering fly?"
"I'm a pirate you fool, now step to the side,
for I've treasure to find, that can no longer hide."
But before the white weasel could slip through the door,
the troll swung his stick, knocking him down to the floor,
"Well first do you have the password to cross?
For that is an issue says Mace who's the boss."
"Well, no, not exactly, maybe I don't,
unless it's *candy corn gumballs* or *marshmallow dough?*"
"I'm afraid that's not it, so get out of my head,
for I'm tired of standing and could use a soft bed,
now go flutter your wings in the opposite way,
and leave me alone on this beautiful day."
Then just as the pirate opened his mouth wide to wail,
Tuffo stepped forward and yanked on his tail,
and greeted the troll who stood solemnly still,
with shoulders straight back like a pickle-nosed dill.

11

"Excuse me my friend but there's no need to get rude,
you seem like a nice fellow and you're a very tall dude,
we're just traveling buddies on a marvelous trip,
so let us pass now without all of this ignorant lip."
Well this shocked the troll who had not even seen,
this tough little creature with one eye it seemed,
so closer he looked at the Loodoodle boy's face,
and a hush filled the air as he gulped down his taste.
"Wait just a second, is that a flower tight patch,
over one of your eyes like a circular scratch?"
"Why yes it sure is but what's the big deal?
Are you teasing my sight which a toucan did steal?
My eye will grow back for I was told that it would,
by a wizard named Manny who said that it could.
Do you hold that against me, my lack of clear sight?
Do you think I look funny and gawk now in spite?"
"No, why of course not, for my job is now through,
I've been waiting for moons on a Loodoodle like you.
for Cora said one day you'd be searching for treasure,
and to finally now meet you is all of my pleasure,
so enter you must and let me be gone,
for I've fruit to go eat by Royal Fish Pond!"
And not an eye in the land had blinked half a lid,
before the troll disappeared and so enter they did,
through the pastel drawn door which blurred yellow to red,
into a butterfly land where Mace sat ahead.
"Welcome !" he said as he leaped off a box,
which had engravings of animals behind golden seal locks,
"I believe that you came here looking for these,"
he said to the group as he carved out some keys.